Mouse In House

Judith Schermer

Houghton Mifflin Company · Boston · 1979

JE
c.2

Library of Congress Cataloging in Publication Data

Schermer, Judith.
  Mouse in house.

  SUMMARY: A family nearly tears the house apart
trying to oust a mouse but their daughter saves the
day with an inventive scheme.
  [1. Family life – Fiction.   2.   Mice – Fiction]
I. Title.
PZ7.S3439Mo   [E]   78-24406

ISBN 0-395-27801-5

For Abigail, Katharine, Sue,
John, Ginny, Ollie,
Pippi, and Aunt Tess

Mama   Dad

House

Baby   Tess

Mouse!

20

24

25